Josiah Hartzell

Sketch of the Life of Mrs. William McKinley

Josiah Hartzell

Sketch of the Life of Mrs. William McKinley

ISBN/EAN: 9783337416539

Printed in Europe, USA, Canada, Australia, Japan

Cover: Foto ©Andreas Hilbeck / pixelio.de

More available books at **www.hansebooks.com**

Sketch of the Life

of

Mrs. William McKinley

BY

JOSIAH HARTZELL, PH. D.

WASHINGTON, D. C.
THE HOME MAGAZINE PRESS.
MDCCCXCVI.

Sketch of the Life

of

Mrs. William McKinley

CHAPTER I.

FATHERS AND MOTHERS.

"Far from the madding crowd's ignoble strife
Their sober wishes never learned to stray;
Along the cool, sequestered vale of life
They kept the even tenor of their way."

VISITORS to Canton, in the State of Ohio, cannot help carrying away with them pleasing memories of the thrifty little city. True, there is no wide expanse of water, no mountain, no level plain. But it is a county seat, and the central mart of a most fertile and fruitful agricultural region. Within its limits two beautiful streams with old Indian names are clasped together and ripple southward to join the brimming river which has christened the famous Commonwealth with its own mellifluous name. Low, forest-tufted hills encircle the city's site, but keep at a respectful distance, their gentle slopes flecked with straight-rowed orchards from whose green bosoms gleam the big, red barns of plenty, and with the deft and varied tilth whereby the old-fashioned, Pennsylvania Dutch farmer knows how to gladden the eye.

Mrs. James A. Saxton.

Mrs. James A. Saxton was the mother of Mrs. William McKinley. She died in 1873.

The city has, they say, about forty thousand inhabitants. It has wide, clean-paved streets, and in respect to the latter-day things that water, steam, gas, and electricity can do, it is, and has, all that science and art can give. The public buildings tower up like exclamation points emphasiz-

(5)

ing the aspect of solid thrift and the go-ahead spirit of the
people.

There is one drawback—about two hundred smoke-stacks
fringe the periphery of the inhabited district. By the help
of the bituminous coals, which are everywhere to be had by
simply digging downwards, these tall chimneys are able to
charge passing air currents with insinuative qualities that knit
the brows of tidy housewives. There is, however, a good deal
of tolerance accorded to the smoke-stacks in their quality as
pioneers of all the other costly improvements, and as the real

The Old Saxton Residence.

This is the old Saxton homestead in which Mrs. McKinley was born and
raised. It was also the temporary home of Major and Mrs. McKinley during
Congressional vacations. It numbers among its guests of former years many
historic names. From its veranda, fronting on the street, General and Senator Sherman, Blaine, Garfield, Hayes, Logan, Vice-president Wilson, Justices
Chase and Matthews, Foraker, Generals Crook and McCook, Hannibal Hamlin,
Col. Fred Grant and Secretary Foster, have been introduced and made speeches
to Canton audiences. This house is now the residence of Mr. and Mrs. Marshall Barber. Mrs. Barber, Mrs. McKinley's sister, has been mistress of the
house since her mother's death, in 1873.

transformers of the beautiful village into the more prosperous
city.

Away back in 1815 the form of Canton's nucleus had been
already marked out by the surveyor. Houses had clustered
about the central square, and street routes pushed their course
out a little way into surrounding thickets of forest and hazel-
brush. There were only a few hundred inhabitants, but the
site was sightly, and the surroundings were full of that good-

ness of promise to the chief county town which has since been so amply justified. Near the end of February in that year, 1815, an ox-team drove up into the square, drawing a wagon upon which stood a strange device—a huge, upright, twisty, clumsy form of iron. From its one side projected an iron track, and from its other side a club-handle of wood—it was the printing press of John Saxton. Nearly three generations have come and gone, but the iron feet of the old press still have their strong grasp on the floor in a corner of the printing establishment which they stoutly carried forward for many, many years.

John Saxton.

John Saxton was for many years known as the Nestor of Ohio editors. He founded the *Ohio Repository* in 1815 and remained its chief until 1871. He was Mrs. McKinley's grandfather.

Saxton got his press and type-boxes into a quickly-built shed of new-sawed boards, and issued his first paper, one of the first in the new State of Ohio, on March 15. Three months after that, to a day, was fought the battle of Waterloo. And three months after that, September 15, the news of Wellington's victory, coming by sail and stage-coach, was printed in Mr. Saxton's "Repository." The particulars of the second Napoleonic Waterloo, of the battle of Sedan, fought September 4, 1870, were also printed by Mr. Saxton, but this time on the evening of the same day.

This curious measure of continuous service has had few parallels, either in respect to duration or the importance of the steps of the world's progress, of which Mr. Saxton's paper had been the witness and the chronicler. Politically, he was first a Whig, then a Republican. Having pitched his tent among a class of people who persisted in voting for Jackson, he was used to defeat. He lived to see a great change, and was himself a chief instrument in bringing it about. He was, during forty years, a Presbyterian elder. Though a man of strong convictions he was universally respected, and counted among his personal friends many of the most illustrious names in our national history. To the writer of this sketch Horace Greeley classed Mr. Saxton as one of the most reliable and consistent advocates of Whig, and subsequently of Republican and Protectionist doctrines in the, then, Western country. Joseph

Medill, the veteran Chicago editor, never approves a sketch of his own life which does not contain a grateful tribute to the old "Repository," in which his boyhood was first made familiar with the current happenings of the world two generations ago. The Medill and Saxton families are related. John Saxton died April 16, 1871. His wife, who was a woman of sterling qualities, and in all respects fitted for the companionship of so worthy a man, had preceded him by thirteen years.

Mrs. George Dewalt.

Mrs. Dewalt was Mrs. McKinley's maternal grandmother. She died in 1869.

James A. Saxton was John Saxton's oldest son, having been born in 1820. After reaching maturity he was engaged in banking, also in large commercial and manufacturing enterprises. He was one of the most prominent and influential men in the region in which he lived. He died in 1887. In 1846 he was married to Miss Kate Dewalt, a lady whose parents were also among the earliest settlers in Canton. By the older residents of Canton no name is more sacredly cherished than that of Mrs. Kate Saxton. Nature had endowed her with the graces of a perfect womanhood, and the home over which she presided was one of the most attractive social centers in the community. The children of Mr. and Mrs. Saxton were George, Ida

James A. Saxton.

Mr. James A. Saxton was Mrs. William McKinley's father. He was one of the most influential and prominent citizens of Canton during his active life. He died in 1887 at the age of 67 years.

—now Mrs. William McKinley—and Mary B., now Mrs. Marshall Barber. All three are residents of Canton at the present time.

A celebrated dictum of Dr. Oliver Wendell Holmes, known to

William McKinley—father.

everyone, ascribes much importance to ante-natal influences. Prompted by this consideration it has been deemed well to present this short preface by way of introduction to the brief sketch of the life of Mrs. William McKinley which occupies the following pages.

> "The times need men—Not those with learning's dower
> And gifts that make them idols of the hour;
> But men whose hearts are true, whose souls are strong
> To breast the current of mistake and wrong."

CHAPTER II.

GIRLHOOD.

"There is a tide in life's great sea
Which ebbs and flows for you and me,
And which, if taken at its flood
Will surely lead us on to good;
But if we wait till it recedes
Our feet may tangle in the weeds,
Then our weak and trembling hands
May never lift us from the sands."

THE loveliest thing in this world is the morning of life of the well-born American girl. I say American girl, because across the sea girlhood is different. There the parental watch-

Miss Ida Saxton, 1868.

fulness of daughters is extreme. The restrictions there put upon the personal liberty of maidens would here be regarded as ridiculous and intolerable.

In well-ordered American homes the girls are taught self-reliance, self-culture, independence. Careful moral training and the lofty ideals set by good mothers lie at the base of a real education that fits them to fight their battles of life and win the victor's crown. It is due to these potent and sturdy influences that our European visitors are compelled to such unanimity in praise of the freshness, the originality, the self-poise, and the surprising beauty of American girls.

Ida Saxton had all these attractions in fullest measure. Her mother, and her mother's mother, who was a member of the family until Ida reached womanhood, both were women noted for their exact appreciation of all the good and gracious domesticities. Under their hands the sweet little English word "home" had its idealized meaning rounded out into most ample proportions. Colleges and seminaries have their place,

(10)

and their good capabilities, but in the construction of character, of a sweet girlhood and a gentle womanhood, all the education they are capable of giving dwindles in comparison with the precept and example of su h a mother as Ida Saxton was blessed with. Good education, or good habits, which are about the same thing, make good deeds easy and bad ones difficult. These were part of her mother's dowry.

Her father lived in a large and easy way. He was of imposing stature physically, and a man of broad mental grasp. In the battle of life he won both distinction and fortune, for his time. He was most indulgent with his household gods ; among whom his beautiful daughter stood on a high pedestal.

Of course Ida went to the city school. The Cantonians are exacting about their schools. For many years their motto has been: The best is not too good. One of her teachers was Betsy Cowles, sister of Edwin Cowles, a noted journalist and founder of the Cleveland "Leader." She was an apt learner,

Mrs. Marshall Barber.

Mrs. Barber is Mrs. McKinley's only sister. Her husband is a manufacturer The Barber family resides in the old Saxton homestead at Canton.

and her advancement speedily warranted the superior advantages offered, first, by a private school at Delhi, New York ; later, by one in Cleveland, and subsequently by Brook Hall Seminary, at Media, Pennsylvania. In the latter institution she spent three happy years. Being a girl of that practical, sound sense which characterized her race and blood, her schooling effectively supplemented her womanly attractions.

A good deal is said and written now-a-days about the college girl. Dry figures even are dragged in to prove that finishing schools cast a mildew over girls' social, at any rate, their matrimonial prospects. The truth may be that this result is after all not so much due to real education as to the lack of it; to half education and its sure sequelæ of conceited pretentiousness. From these blemishes Ida Saxton was absolutely free. Character building with her had been plain, unvarnished, solid. When she left Media she was as she is to-day, the perfect type of candor and womanly independence.

In the summer of 1869 Miss Saxton and her sister Miss Mary
B. Saxton constituted part of a group of young ladies who
made a European tour. Made under expert guidance, as this
trip was, the memory treasures gathered constitute a per-
petual source of pleasure to their possessor, and of interest to

First Methodist Church of Canton.

Governor and Mrs. McKinley have been members of this congregation many years.
He was at one time superintendent of the Sunday School. He is now a trustee.

her associates. The return to America was in the fall of the same
year. With her she brought presents gathered in foreign lands for
each of the two dozen boys and girls who constituted her Sunday school class. These presents are now exhibited by grown-
up people as souvenirs with no little exultation. Some of her
boy scholars have become men of prominence and naturally,
stand high in the Governor's favor.

During a few succeeding years Miss Saxton was, as the lawyers would say, very much in evidence in the social life of Canton. She was young, beautiful, high-minded, independent, and her equipment of wit and repartee assured to her the quick respect and profound deference of all her associates. We will not try to depict the lights and shadows, the varying experiences of this iridescent period, for both lights and shadows there must be in every picture. But in her case there could have been no shadow of any serious disappointment, for she was easily, and in every respect, the most attractive figure in the social life of the little city. Religiously she belonged to the Presbyterian flock.

Part of these years she spent in the Stark County Bank which belonged to her father. As a matter of fact she could, and did, run the bank on occasion. It was a diversion; and was besides in line with the craving to be helpful, which is the quality of a wholesome, healthful character.

The bees and the birds have their places, and in the easy-going old Dutch town of Canton the young gentlemen had the bank wicket. "The Traditions of the Wicket" might constitute a graceful chapter of this history had they not all faded from memory—all but one.

That one has to do with the boyish face and figure of a singularly handsome young man. To see him no one would have suspected that he had already tramped the weary hills of Virginia four years through the smoke of war in defence of his country. Soldier as he was, he flitted before the wicket and was made tight and fast. Pleasure drivers to the woods and lakes began to see these two in the lover's lanes—there were really three, but the little winged attendant kept discreetly out of view. In front of Mr. Saxton's house was a wide porch screened from the street by a net-work of curiously twisted vines. Through the meshes of these vines the other wicket-haunters began to see visions that induced in them a pale cast of thought.

In every maiden's life there comes a day hazy with enchanting mysteries. Reveries of future bliss enshroud even the pitfalls that may yawn before her forward step. In such a moment one man's opinion of another man may be of priceless value to her. By this time James A. Saxton knew Major McKinley well. He had the clear vision of a practiced man of

affairs.   His joyful consent and his father's blessing dispelled
the mists of doubt, if any there were, and left his daughter
enveloped in the pure white sunlight of a perfect and loving
faith.   Mr. Saxton lived to see the day when his son-in-law
became his own strong right arm, and the farther day when he
had already centered upon himself the approving admiration of
his countrymen.

At the time we were speaking of a moment ago the handsome

Presbyterian Church.
This is the church in which Major and Mrs. McKinley were married.

ex-soldier was superintendent of the Methodist Sunday school.
At the quadrennial conference of that church held last May
at Cleveland, Ohio, an attending minister penciled on his knee
an incident that he had just heard.   The editor of one of the
"Advocates" sat just in front of him.   He passed his little
sheet over to him with this whisper: "Here is an item for your
paper." It read thus:

"Nothing more romantic and beautiful in the matter of courtship has ever been published than the courtship of the next President with the lovely woman who is now his wife. In Canton, the town where they resided, she was teacher of a large Bible class in the First Presbyterian Church and he the superintendent of the Sunday school of the First Methodist Episcopal Church. In going to their respective schools they passed each other at a certain corner, and found it pleasant to stop occasionally and indulge in conversation concerning their work. This went on for many months, until, on an ever memorable Sunday afternoon in their history, he said to her:

"I don't like this separation every Sunday, you going one way and I another. Let us change the order. Suppose after this we always go the same way. I think that is the thing for us to do. What do you think?"

"I think so, too," was the answer, which gave him the most beautiful of wives and her one of the noblest and most devoted of husbands.

> "If there be a human tear
> From passion's dross refined and clear,
> 'Tis that which pious fathers shed
> Upon a duteous daughter's head."
> —[Lady of the Lake.]

CHAPTER III.

SUNSHINE AND ECLIPSE.

"A good woman is the loveliest flower that blooms under heaven, and we look with love and wonder upon its silent grace, its pure fragrance, its delicate bloom of beauty, sweet and beautiful! The fairest and the most spotless! Is it not a pity to see them bowed down, or devoured by grief inexorable, wasting in disease, pining with long pain, or cut off suddenly in their prime? We may deserve grief, but why should women be unhappy? Except that we know that Heaven chastens those whom it loves best; being pleased by repeated trials to make their pure spirits more pure."—Thackeray.

THIS is to be a chapter of pleasure and pain; of joy and sorrow. Of joys as great as mortal can safely endure,

United States Capitol.

and of sorrows greater still, for they crushed the soul and pressed the stricken body well nigh into the grave.

Ida Saxton was now Mrs. William McKinley, Jr. They had taken the marriage vow on January 25th, 1871, the ceremony being held in the Presbyterian Church. The new and handsome church building had just been completed and the

(16)

wedding was in the nature of a dedicatory service in more
senses than one. The acquaintance of the bride and groom
was large and the church was jammed. The writer of this
was the reporter of that occasion, and he has before him his
own somewhat lengthy account of the wedding. The local
particulars would not interest the reader. Heart of lover and
beloved could wish for nothing more gracious or beauteous.
It is proper to say here that while Mrs. McKinley had been of
her family's, the Presbyterian faith, after her marriage she
became a communicant of the Methodist Church to which her

These are small photos of Major and Mrs. McKinley taken in January, 1871, in New
York City, during their wedding trip. This pair, neatly framed, constitutes one of Mrs.
McKinley's highly-prized parlor decorations.

husband belonged. After the wedding the newly-married
couple took instant flight, as usual. In order to be by themselves they went to the crowded cities of the East.

On their return home from their wedding trip they at once
as the saying is, set up housekeeping. They gathered together
their household gods and set them up around the fireside in
the house in which they live to-day. That house is now the
Mecca of the hopes and aspirations of the powerful political
party which has controled the destinies of the United States
almost continuously since the year 1861. It is the party which
conquered the rebellion, freed the slave, restored the Union,

and which has given to history many of the most honored and
illustrious names in modern times.   To have conferred such a
distinction on the house in which he lives it is easy to infer that
the handsome soldier boy who was caught and held fast by
a pair of blue eyes peering through the little bank-wicket
must have been disporting himself somewhat conspicuously
over the high arena of the great American Nation.

Such has indeed been the case, and some note has got to be
made of the matter in order to make this history intelligible.
It can as well be done right now ; but it must be done rather
grudgingly, for there are already whole libraries about Major
McKinley, while ours is only to be one little booklet about
Mrs. McKinley.

During the first six years after his marriage Major McKinley
had the ups and downs that befall a young lawyer.   The
average grade was up, and at a sharp angle.   In 1876 he was
elected to Congress where his district kept him steadily and
busily employed until 1891.   Perhaps it would be more correct
to say that he kept himself well employed, for his grade mark
in Congress was also continuously upward, and also at a sharp
angle.   During his last term he was chairman of the Ways
and Means Committee, the most conspicuous station on the
floor of the House of Representatives.   The law bearing his
name was the most important measure passed by Congress
since the war.

In 1891, a year noted for wide-spread relapse to Democracy,
he was elected Governor of Ohio by 26,000 majority ; in 1893
he was re-elected by over 80,000 majority.   To all the high
offices which he has filled with such striking tokens of public
approbation he had been nominated by acclamation.   He was
recognized as the most formidable champion, and the most
powerful defender of distinctively Republican principles.   The
climax of his career was his almost unanimous nomination for
President by the National Republican Convention at St. Louis
on June 18th, 1896.   The reader now understands why the
McKinley residence has been spoken of as the Republican
Mecca.

And now, to go back : In 1871 this house was the home of as
devoted a pair of lovers as can be produced from the pages of
any poem or novel.   Their future was radiant with the promise
of every joy.   Both were healthy, handsome ; both of pioneer

American stock with marked records for longevity. His boy-soldier history gave him a title to consideration possessed by few of his age. Both were well educated; well enough to know that real education is without set bounds, and that school time should last while life lasts. The Major's scholastic drill had been peculiar. While others of his age were following Xenophon and Cæsar, he trudged his way up and down the Virginias. His Xenophon and Cæsar were Grant and Sheridan. He had no Greek dictionary, but he had a well-worn knapsack and a good musket. His college was the tented field; his recitations were made under the smoky canopy of battle. His diploma was an honor to himself and it was satisfactory to his young wife. Both were social favorites. They were not rich; though if wealth could have taken measure in lofty resolves Major McKinley would have been a rich man from the start. Gold and bonds would have shriveled all that; he was most fortunate in his poverty.

The first event to ruffle the even flow and tenor of the new

Katie McKinley

household was Heaven's best gift to deserving young parents — a baby. That was Christmas day, 1871. The baby was christened Katie, after Mrs. McKinley's mother. About thirteen months afterwards, April 1, 1873, the family circle received another addition; another little girl who got the name of Ida. Under favoring auspices the young mother's cup of happiness would have been full to overflowing. She has always loved children. The maternal instinct in her betrays itself with smiles

Notification Committee— Photographe

he Porch of Major McKinley's Home

and goodness on every occasion. If more kindly stars could
only have beamed upon the destiny of these children, and upon
her own life, what a world of sorrow might have been averted,
and how great might have been her joy !

Mrs. McKinley had already tasted the bitterness of final
parting from loved ones. Her grandfather Saxton and her
grandmother Dewalt, most lovable people, in whose close companionship she had grown to womanhood, both had passed
away; the one a short time before, and the other a few months
after her marriage. In March, 1873, less than fifteen months
after the birth of her first child, her own mother died. She,
herself, was the oldest daughter—daughter and almost sister.
Many who read this have seen their mothers consigned to the
narrow house. They know what it means. Others do not,
and cannot.

New and still graver trials awaited the young mother. The
ligament of love that unites parent to child is much the largest
at the parent end. The shock of its severance is proportion-
ately greater. In August, 1873, the baby, Ida, was borne to
the cemetery. She was a little less than five months old. To

Residence of Governor McKinley's Mother.

the great world the sweet little baby had no history; but in
her mother's memory treasure-house she was a jewel far above
all this earth had ever seen. In June, 1876, Katie, the first-
born, was laid in her bed of earth along side the grassy mound
of her baby sister. Katie was three years and a half old, to a

day. Her identity was established. Her traits, her promise, could be seen. She was sweet and good, and centered upon her golden head the rays of unbounded love.

These cruel separations, coming one after another in quick succession, prostrated Mrs. McKinley so that for many months her own life hung suspended on a very slender thread. Her nervous system, most sensitive and high strung, was almost wrecked. The wounds upon her heart have never been fully healed. The most eminent specialists have failed to restore the equipoise of perfect health. There is no defined malady or disease; none of the irritability of feeble selfishness or prostration. When the enchanting dream of life in the companionship of her cherished babes was obscured by the sharp, quick eclipse of death she reeled and fell, it is true, but into strong and loving arms, where, cradled by patience and goodness beyond the reach of words, and soothed by the healing hand of time, she has been restored to the shining circle of those she had held most dear.

> " We do not know the value of our grief
> Till we look back upon it from afar,
> And then, when time has given us relief,
> It shines upon us like a quiet star."

CHAPTER IV

FOUNDATIONS OF FAITH.

"The heights by great men reached and kept
Were not attained by sudden flight,
But they, while their companions slept,
Were toiling upward in the night."

—[Longfellow.]

STRICKEN by cruel bereavement, as Mrs. McKinley has been, and with physical strength so impaired that she has not, for a score of years, walked without assistance, it is still not impossible, but probable, that she may have been an

Ohio State Capitol.

important factor in the equipment of the man who now seems destined to be the next ruler of the American Nation. Her husband is already the nominee of his party for President. The campaign of the candidates was most interesting, and disclosed the fact that Major McKinley was everywhere the popular favorite. He was not the choice of the professional politicians—most of that class were his avowed opponents. He was without family or other prestige more than falls to the lot of any American born of industrious, God-fearing parents. He had been a soldier, but his highest military grade was comparatively humble. He lived in hotels and had no wealth, no sumptuous establishment which enabled him to entertain and impress the social world. He had only his invalid wife and himself.

It is true that his devotion to his wife has few parallels. It has been unceasingly, sensitively watchful. None could see, or know of it, without being touched. A strong admiration for him would be the inevitable result. This nation is made up, not only of Republicans and Democrats; of protectionists and free-traders. It is made up of parents and children, of husbands and wives. Human nature, human goodness, consecration, self-sacrifice, open the door to our favor; at the very least they oil the hinges, however rusted with prejudices and partisanisms.

In all the annals of chivalry there is no more beautiful example of manly self-sacrifice and of womanly gratefulness. This domestic state, however, could not be utilized as an object lesson. It was too sacred a thing, in anybody's case, to be bandied about in the public prints. Nevertheless, in these newspaper times, it was inevitable that it should get into print; but for the honor of the press it must be said that these things have only been alluded to with the greatest respect, even by Major McKinley's political opponents. A sketch of Mrs. McKinley must have some reference to this circumstance, especially since the nomination; after the election, and in farther remote years, it will be sure to have a place among the most gracious traditions incidental to the private life of American Presidents.

The personal circle of those who could have been thus directly influenced was necessarily comparatively small at best. The wide-spread favor of the people toward Major McKinley is more largely due to something else; is due, in fact, to his achievements as a legislator, and to his powerful advocacy of political principles and methods on the public forums of the Nation. The preparation for such labors as he has accomplished, necessarily presupposes seclusion, exhaustive study and profound thought.

Excepting during the occupancy of his seat in the sessions of Congress Mrs. McKinley has been at her husband's side during all his public life. He has thus been spared the exhausting and time-consuming inroads made on the lives of

public men by the exactions of modern society life.   Her education, reading, temperament and perspicacity eminently fitted
her for his useful and helpful companionship.   He was a great
social favorite, but he needed no other society ; his place was
at her side.   And it was there, in that pure atmosphere, sanc-
tified by love, by sorrow, and by supremest devotion that Major
McKinley built the foundations of that faith in himself, of that
stately reputation for patriotic statesmanship, which assures to
him the highest token of approbation within the gift of a free
people.

The comforts of modern travel permit Mrs. McKinley to ac-

Major and Mrs. McKinley.
From a photograph taken in San Francisco in 1881.

company her husband wherever she desires to go.   Journeying
agrees with her and she takes great delight in it, both by reason
of the ever changing scenes and experiences thus afforded, and
of her lively pleasure in witnessing the distinguished honors
which are showered upon her husband in every part of the
land.   Mrs. McKinley is quite capable of making his friends
her friends.   She has assisted at very many crowded receptions,
often as the central figure, and if she becomes the mistress of the

White House she will probably be able to recognize as large a circle of personal acquaintances as any lady who has ever presided over the Executive Mansion.

Her philosophy will make her fully equal to the demands imposed by the more exalted station to which she may be called. These demands could not well be greater then than now.

She has thousands of visitors. To callers she makes no secret of her physical weakness, but smilingly points to her nearby gold-headed cane as one of her fast friends. In close proximity also are two little rocking chairs, her Katie's, and that of her own babyhood, which bring the heads of her little visitors just high enough to get an affectionate caress from her beautiful white hand. She talks well and listens well. Her manner is so natural and unrestrained that the visitor is sure to carry away a most

Mrs. William McKinley
Photographed at Columbus, O., during her husband's term as Governor.

gentle memory of her ; and it will not be her fault if this good opinion fails to include within its span the Republican candidate for the Presidency of the Nation.

It can be taken for granted that the illustrations contained in this booklet will gratify the wishes of those who desire a satisfactory impression in regard to Mrs. McKinley's personality. It is true that certain writers endeavor, by printed words and phrasings, to depict her features and peculiarities. Such descriptions leave only a confused idea, or no idea at all, of personal appearance, while photo-engravings, such as are found in these pages, speak so instantly and clearly to the eye as to leave nothing more or better to be desired.

Her life is already gracefully tinted with embellishments derived from White House experiences. She was the most intimate friend and confidante of the wife of President Hayes. She often presided at the White House during the absence of the President's family. Another member of President Hayes' family was Miss Platt, the attractive niece of Mrs. Hayes These three ladies were much together. President Hayes and Major McKinley were, themselves, on that brotherly footing engendered during their campaigns in the Twenty-third Ohio regiment.

This interesting group, three ladies and two gentlemen, lacked equilibrium. This defect was remedied by General Russell Hastings who, by the consent of Miss Platt, was accorded a place on the scales. General Hastings was also of the Twenty-Third Ohio, and had had his hero-metal tested by battle, involving every sacrifice but life. The trysting place of these lovers was the drawing room of Mrs. McKinley at her hotel. They were married in the White House. If the people's will places Major and Mrs McKinley in the president's house, those same people will by no means be offended if they see, among the near and close intimates of the president's family, the dignified form of the tall, lame man who was mowed to the earth by the iron hail at the Sheridan battle of Winchester, and of his lovely wife, the niece of Lucy Webb Hayes.

After fourteen years' almost continuous residence in Washington, Major and Mrs. McKinley spent about a year in Canton. During this period political campaigning made heavy drafts on the Major's time, and his absences were many and prolonged. Fortunately for Mrs. McKinley, there was waiting for her a home such as she could most have desired, in the house in which she was born and raised. The heads of the family were Mr. and Mrs. Marshall Barber, who are the owners of the old family homestead. Mrs. Barber, as before stated, is Mrs. McKinley's only sister. Her only brother, Mr. George D. Saxton, a bachelor gentleman, is also a member of the family.

Mrs. Barber has, in certain respects, been more favored than her sister, first by good health ; she is also the mother of seven children. Several of these are old enough to be in attendance at college. The oldest daughter, Miss Mary, is a beautiful young lady, and when at home, is very often seen near her aunt. During his last year at Columbus Governor McKinley made a tour of the State for the purpose of reviewing the several camps of the Ohio National Guard. By invitation of the Governor and his wife, Miss Barber, Miss Grace McKinley, the Governor's niece, and a number of other highly-favored young ladies, were of the party. The newspapers of the State vied with each other in saying finest things about the attract-

WILLIAM MCKINLEY.

ive character of the escort with which the Governor and his wife had provided themselves. Mrs. McKinley takes a deep interest in the welfare of her sister's children, and her temporary home among them was greatly enjoyed. Not infrequently she gratified her fondness for the nearness of the little ones, by having some of the younger members of her sister's flock in her own circle during her residence at Columbus, which extended from January 1891, to January 1895.

" No radiant pearl which crested fortune wears,
No gem that twinkling hangs from beauty's ears,
Not the bright stars which night's blue arch adorn,
Nor rising sun that gilds the vernal morn,
Shine with such lustre as the tear that flows
Down virtue's manly cheek for other's woes."
—[Dr. Darwin.]

CHAPTER V.

APOTHEOSIS OF HOME.

"Home is where the heart is,
In dwelling great or small;
There is many a stately mansion,
That's never a home at all."

PRETTY stories about the lovers get wings, such as that of the sly reporter who surprised their signal line between the State House grounds and a hotel window which

Residence of Governor and Mrs. McKinley

This is the house in which they commenced their married life, and in which they now live. The lawn in front was a handsome green, until June 18th, the day of Governor McKinley's nomination at St. Louis. The visiting crowds on that day destroyed the grass, flower-beds, and a considerable portion of the fence. Delegations from various parts of the country visit this place daily. The speeches are from the front porch. Those of Senator Thurston, Chairman of the Notification Committee, and Governor McKinley's response, on June 25th, have been the most noted, thus far.

served as the invalid's watch-tower : also that of the eleven-year-old Buckeye girl who snatched off her red petticoat and safely signaled from certain destruction a train carrying Frenchmen to the Chicago World's Fair, and who, through their, and the interposition of the Governor's household, got the cross of the Legion of Honor from the president of the

French Republic. Mrs. McKinley's more amiable weaknesses are children, flowers, and fine needle-work. There are in several cities gentle legends of a White Lady who stops her carriage and calls to her side little ones that have attracted her attention ; also of pretty gifts, made by her own hands, distributed among the "administration babies" or the tender bairns of her husband's official family. And there are other stories, true ones, which show a calm strength where strong men have wavered, a will of finely-tempered steel to brave impending calamity. The flowers are nearest of kin. They are with her always. Last fall the Governor was on one of his famous tours, speaking at every station. In Iowa one morning he addressed several acres of people from the rear of his car, then sat down to breakfast. He heard the clatter and clamor of little girls trying to reach him. He came to their rescue and was rewarded by a big bunch of flowers. Turning to his secretary he said : "Smith, take those posies, especially the wild ones, wrap them in wet cloth and express them to Mrs. McKinley with a tag telling her how I came by them." That incident needs no comment.

After the nomination the Tippecanoe Club of Cleveland sent her a basket of roses four feet square bearing this inscription : "With congratulations on the nomination of your noble husband to the highest office in the gift of the American people."

There is in Canton a Flower Mission—a mission of young ladies aiming to soften the hard asperities of hospital life. Sweet flowers and sweeter charity walk hand in hand. Mrs. McKinley's nieces are members, and she is a fervent patroness of this charming guild.

Many of the nobler traits of Governor McKinley's character were made conspicuously obvious during his two terms as Governor of Ohio. During this period his extraordinary legislative record was supplemented by a no less brilliant career as the Executive Chief of one of the foremost commonwealths in the Union. The great favor with which he was regarded was the source of intensest delight to that most fragile and dependent lady, who lived, moved, and had her being in him.

The functions of a Governor are to some extent of a social character and, thanks to her constantly, though slowly improving health and strength, she was better able to enter into the spirit and enjoyment of these phases of her husband's life than she had ever been in Washington.

As the wife of the Chief Magistrate, she did her part, and

Mrs. Nancy McKinley,

Mother of Governor McKinley. She was born at New Lisbon, Ohio, in 1809. Her maiden name was Allison, the family being related to that of Senator Allison, of Iowa.

did it well. They had their home in a hotel, as usual. In their spacious apartments she was always accessible, and her circle of friendships was greatly enlarged. The first hotel in which they lived was burned during one of their absences. While the destruction was almost complete, the personal effects of Mrs. McKinley were saved with comparatively little loss. She had endeared herself to the hotel people, as she does to all who come within the sphere of her influence, and their first thought was to rescue from the flames the things held dear by the Governor's good wife. She can well be pardoned for the exquisitely grateful terms in which she refers to this instance of personal devotion, and perhaps of self-sacrifice, on the part of her friends.

Miss Grace McKinley.

During their stay at Columbus, visits to Canton were much more frequent than during their residence in Washington, and they generally stopped with the Governor's mother. This lady, now in her 88th year, is a widow, her husband having died three years ago. Her family consists of her daughter, Miss Helen McKinley, a grandson of sixteen, and Miss Grace McKinley, who was mentioned in a previous chapter. The two last named are orphans, who have been taken into the protecting home and guardianship of their grandmother. On holidays, and on her anniversary days, Governor and Mrs. McKinley were quite sure to be seen at Grandmother McKinley's, by which name she is familiarly known to all her townspeople. Notwithstanding her great age, reaching within twelve years of a century's span, she is in the enjoyment of good health, adequate strength, and she is a delighted witness of the passing events which shed such renown on her illustrious son.

The house in which Major and Mrs. McKinley commenced housekeeping immediately after their marriage was sold after he went to Congress. Happily, it was unoccupied and available for them on his retirement from the Governorship. They took immediate possession and were very soon engaged in making preparations for the proper celebration of their silver wedding anniversary, which occurred on January 25th, 1896. Mrs. McKinley had looked forward to this occasion with a spirit brimfull of gratitude and thankfulness.

True, the old home had upon it the shadow of sorrowful memories, but the healing balm of time had worked its cure for a score of years, during which the grass rootlets also, had woven a thick carpet of green over the resting places of the loved ones. And her own broken and fragile frame, snatched from death's door, and, during all these years, caressed by infinite love and goodness, had been restored to an ever widening circle of joy, and of friends. Friends of her young girlhood, school friends, friends from the familiar places at Washington, friends who gladdened her fireside under the protecting shadows of Ohio's Capitol, many near and dear friends from Cleveland. For representatives of all these saluted her with felicitations and good wishes on the occasion of her silver anniversary. Her assistants comprised the nearer group of relatives, her own and her husband's, already named, and others. The silver wedding was all that heart could wish—Canton had never seen its like.

The home-coming from Columbus was a deeply interesting episode in the life of the McKinley family. They gravitated back to Canton realizing that "Home is where the heart is." For some time previously both husband and wife had pressed their nearer friends, discreetly and in an undertone of apprehension, for an opinion as to the Governor's likelihood of regaining his lost clientele. To be sure the newspapers were already canvassing the candidates, but on his part—on their part—there was no air of assumption. Neither one of them ever dropped a word, either about themselves or others, other candidates included, the recalling of which could cause them the slightest embarrassment. Apparently they had come home to stay.

Politics are uncertain; perhaps Governor McKinley did dream of winning fortune and fame over the trial-table in the courts of justice. If he did, the dream had a rude, quick awakening. For they had hardly been well settled in their new house when the nominating campaign burst forth into wildest fury. In the space of a few weeks it had compelled the

McKinley house to put on somewhat the air of political head-
quarters. Postmen groaned under their loads. Noted men
came daily. Place was made for a long-distance telephone
in one end of the dining-room. Private secretary, stenog-
rapher and type-writers monopolized the largest upstairs
room. The Governor's office is at the right on entering the
lower hall. At the left is a large and handsomely furnished
suite, consisting of a commodious and elegant parlor, and the
private rooms of the family. These rooms are sacred to Mrs.

Miss Mary Barber

McKinley. After the assembling
of the Convention, place had to be
made in the upper hall for an instrument connected by private wire
to the hall of the St. Louis Convention.

About 5 o'clock, June 18th, the
last day of the Convention, the
operator at the wire called down-
stairs announcing that Senator
Thurston, chairman of the Convention, had ordered the roll-call of
the States. Mrs. McKin ey sat in
the parlor surrounded by a group of
friends. The Governor and a few of his own friends occupied his
office. Half a hundred neighbors, mostly provided with score-
cards of States, sat on, or near, the front porch. An attendant
called out the votes of the States from "Alabama" downward,
so that all could hear. When "Ohio" was reached the ag-
gregate for McKinley fell only a few votes short of the number
required to nominate. The solid vote of Ohio completed the
work, and William McKinley stood forth the choice and
nominee of the National Republican party for the office of
President of the United States. The Governor crossed the
hall, and going up to the group of ladies, kissed his wife and
his mother.

Of course there was a rush of feet to reach the man of the
hour and be among the earliest to offer congratulations. Those
present expected to see a lull in this interesting ceremony as
soon as they had finished taking the Governor by the hand.
But on looking out toward the street there was to be seen the

swiftly coming advance column of a hurrying, perspiring crowd no man could number. Bells, steam whistles and the boom of cannon, had heralded the surely expected news, as certainly as if written against the sky, that the soldier boy of Canton, who, thirty years ago, was a youth to fortune and to fame unknown, had been nominated by a powerful political party as its first choice as the ruler of the foremost Nation in the world. Forty minutes later came a train of over twenty crowded cars from Alliance, a neighboring city on the east ; a few minutes after that a still larger crowd from Massillon, a city on the west, and at 7 o'clock, a train of forty-one cars loaded with 3,500 visitors from Akron, twenty-five miles to the north. There were speeches, and music, and speeches. The blaze of colored lights filled the sky, and the air was discordant with rasping sounds far into the night.

It must not be supposed that, during the first period of this generous human effervescence, the heroine of our story had been forgotten or neglected. The better-half of the man whose name rode upon every echo, still occupied her central place in her group of friends. Portraits of her little daughter, of her father and mother, of President and Mrs. Hayes, and others whose memories were part and parcel with her own life, smiled at her from the walls. The venerable form of the Governor's mother presided benignantly over the scene.

In between the black ranks of men many ladies found their winding way to reach the women of the household. A long procession of ladies and gentlemen streamed in and out of the parlor. All were graciously received, and all wore pleased faces. Naturally, the centers of attraction were the Governor's aged mother, and the sweet-faced woman who everyone believed would be established in the White House as the First Lady of the Land.

While all this was going on below the tune played upon the wire in the upper hall had undergone a great change. The Convention was over. From all over our broad land, and from friends across the seas, came the swift, warm words of felicitation. From the Governor's wire, and from the down-town offices, the telegraph poured forth its torrent of yellow slips, harbingers of the joy of the people, until late in the night. Not from men alone, to the Governor, but from men and

women to Mrs. McKinley ; from friends she had known, and
from another multitude of those whose hearts had been melted
by the pathos of her story, and in whose aspirations her husband's name stood transfigured as the symbol of deliverance
and hope.

Scenes of the character shown in picture on preceding page, are very frequently to be witnessed in front of the McKinley house, which stands about 80 feet from the street. Three or four delegations, coming from points in Ohio and other States, often call upon the Governor daily. At times the dense crowds pack the street and yard; the latter has lost its pretty coating of green.

The delegation which is being addressed by the Governor, as shown in the picture, came from Niles, the village in which he was born. The exchange of sentiments was full of feeling on both sides. A peculiar interest was added to this occasion by the attendance, among the delegates, of a large number of the hands from the tin-plate works at Niles, an establishment that was brought into existence by the McKinley law. They bore a number of tin banners with unique inscriptions.

A number of passers-by seemed to have tarried for a moment, and the day being propitious the artist has been able to produce a pretty picture.

POSTSCRIPT.

SINCE the last line of our booklet was written, and while waiting for the printer's proofs and the engraver's pictures, a world of things has happened. The crowds keep coming; delegates representing themselves and others, and visitors with congratulations. The tramp of many feet has left its imprint on the front yard. The pretty coverlet of green has been folded up and spirited away, leaving only an expanse of bare, well-trodden earth. Mrs. McKinley's beds and bands of flowers are only a memory.

The most noteworthy of these visiting bodies was the Notification Committee, appointed by the St. Louis Convention to formally apprise Governor McKinley of his nomination. There was one member for each State. The visit of the Committee was made June 22. Senator Thurston was the spokesman. His speech, and the response of Governor McKinley, were delivered on the front porch. Near by sat the Governor's wife and mother, Mrs. Thurston, and the wives of other members of the Committee. After partaking of a collation, which had been spread in a tent for the visiting parties, the great outside crowd had the pleasure of hearing many short, but eloquent speeches from various members of the Committee. At the end, the photographer begged for a moment of quiet in which he took the picture of the Committee presented on another page.

When not occupied in receiving or addressing callers, the Governor, accompanied by Mrs. McKinley, may be seen almost any day, taking an airing for the latter's health, in what the reporters are pleased to call his "modest" carriage. The expression may correctly be taken as indicating the absence of the pretentious style, liveries, etc., with which people of prominence often provide themselves.

Many of the large newspapers have their special representatives in Canton, whose printed letters are generally characterized by great correctness and ability. Others revel in imaginary things and occasionally give out that the Republican candidate and his wife are going to spend a time at the seaside, or in this, or that city or resort. Thus far in life they have never had either the time, money, or disposition for that class of indulgences. Undoubtedly they will keep to the even tenor of their way right here in Canton until duty shall point out another path.

Speaking of duty suggests this query : shutting politics with its din and fury out of the question, how could all that is good, and pure, and gracious in American life and tradition more truly honor itself, and be honored, than for a Free People by its free voice to invite this great and good statesman to exchange his vine-clad cottage for a temporary residence in its White House at Washington ? But no horoscope of his future, no vista of "pleasures and palaces," would have any charm for him unless his better-half was at his side, whether his lot be cast in vine-clad cottage, or in the official home of the ruler of that Free People in whose public service the best years of his life have been spent.